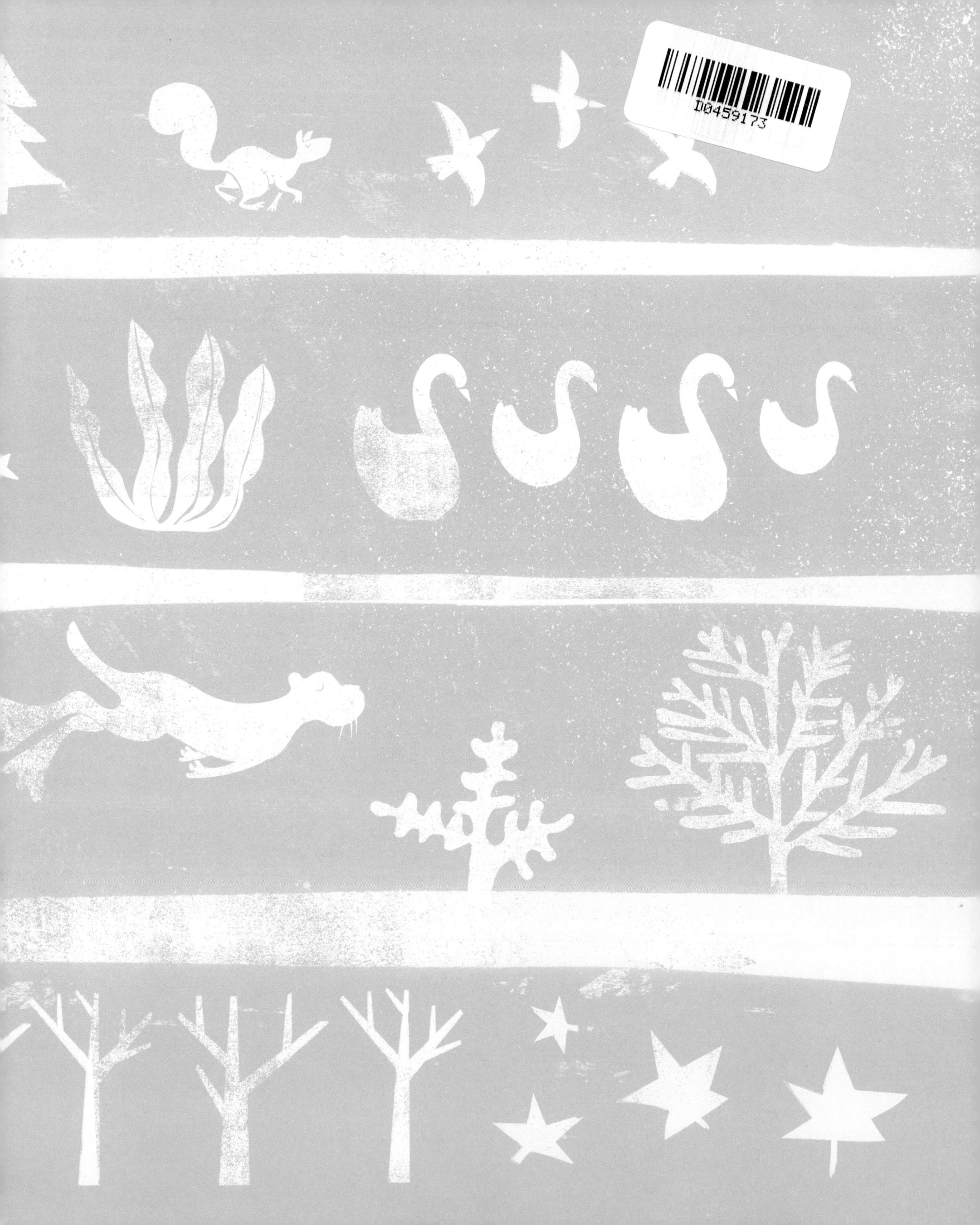

DINO
duckling

For different ducks everywhere
A.M.

Little, Brown and Company
Hachette Book Group
1290 Avenue of the Americas, New York, NY 10104
Visit us at LBYR.com

Originally published in October 2017 by Hachette Children's Group in Great Britain
First U.S. Edition: January 2018

Little, Brown and Company is a division of Hachette Book Group, Inc.
The Little, Brown name and logo are trademarks of Hachette Book Group, Inc.

The publisher is not responsible for websites (or their content) that are not owned by the publisher.

Library of Congress Control Number: 2017941799

ISBNs: 978-0-316-51313-5 (hardcover), 978-0-316-51310-4 (ebook),
978-0-316-51314-2 (ebook), 978-0-316-51311-1 (ebook)

Printed in China

APS

10 9 8 7 6 5 4 3 2 1

The illustrations for this book were created with screenprinting and digital.
The book was printed on 140gsm woodfree paper. The text was set in HVD Bodedo.

DINO
duckling

Alison Murray

LB

LITTLE, BROWN AND COMPANY

NEW YORK   BOSTON

Even as an egg,
Dino Duckling was different.

TAP
TAP

CRACK

BOOM BOOM BOOM CRUNCH

Dino Duckling started out big,

and then he **grew,**

and **grew,**

and **and . . .**

GREW.

Sometimes Dino Duckling
couldn't help feeling different,
but Mama Duck always said,

"Big and wide,
sleek and slim,
we're a family
and we all fit in."

Different didn't make
any difference to her.

As spring turned to summer, Mama Duck taught her babies everything they needed to know.

How to **swim,**

how to **fish,**

how to **share**,

how to navigate
by the **stars**,

and how to
look out
for one another.

Most importantly, she taught them how to **celebrate their differences.**

Sadly, not everyone
thought Dino Duckling belonged.
Sometimes **different** was ...

But Mama Duck just
gathered her babies
close and told them,

"Scales or feathers, big or small, we're a family and there's room for us all."

Summer turned to autumn, and soon it was time to fly south to the sunshine.

Dino Duckling **ran,**

and **jumped,**

and **flapped** . . .

But it was no good. Try as he might,
he simply **couldn't fly.**

Difference does matter,
thought Dino Duckling sadly.

As the leaves blew all around him, Dino Duckling lay down in the reeds and wept.

He imagined his
family far away.

But when he opened his eyes,
Dino Duckling got a
BIG surprise!
He saw . . .

1,2,3,4
faces he recognized!

They were all there.
The **WHOLE** family.

"We would
NEVER leave
without you,"
said Mama Duck.

"Fly or not,
it's all okay.
We're a family,
so we'll find a way."

And they did!